Beck
and the
Great
Berry
Battle

Beck
and the
Great
Berry Battle

WRITTEN BY
Laura Driscoll

ILLUSTRATED BY
Judith Holmes Clarke
& THE DISNEY STORYBOOK ARTISTS

A STEPPING STONE BOOK™
RANDOM HOUSE 🏠 NEW YORK

Library of Congress Cataloging-in-Publication Data

Driscoll, Laura.
Beck and the great berry battle / written by Laura Driscoll;
illustrated by Judith Holmes Clarke.
p. cm.
"A Stepping Stone book."
SUMMARY: Beck, a fairy, has a talent for talking to animals,
but that may not be enough when she tries to mediate a
war between the hummingbirds and the chipmunks.

ISBN 0-7364-2373-7 (pbk.)

[1. War—Fiction. 2. Reconciliation—Fiction. 3. Fairies—Fiction.
4. Chipmunks—Fiction. 5. Hummingbirds—Fiction.]
I. Clarke, Judith, ill. II. Title.
PZ7.D79Be 2006   [Fic]—dc22
2005004837

www.randomhouse.com/kids/disney
Printed in the United States of America
10 9 8 7 6 5 4 3 2 1

All About Fairies

IF YOU HEAD toward the second star on your right and fly straight on till morning, you'll come to Never Land, a magical island where mermaids play and children never grow up.

When you arrive, you might hear something like the tinkling of little bells. Follow that sound and you'll find Pixie Hollow, the secret heart of Never Land.

A great old maple tree grows in Pixie Hollow, and in it live hundreds of fairies and sparrow men. Some of them can do water magic, others can fly like the wind, and still others can speak to animals. You see, Pixie Hollow is the Never fairies' kingdom, and each fairy who lives there has a special, extraordinary talent.

Not far from the Home Tree, nestled in the branches of a hawthorn, is Mother Dove, the most magical creature of all. She sits on her egg, watching over the fairies, who in turn watch over her. For as long as Mother Dove's egg stays well and whole, no one in Never Land will ever grow old.

Once, Mother Dove's egg *was* broken. But we are not telling the story of the egg here. Now it is time for Beck's tale. . . .

Beck
and the
Great
Berry
Battle

1

A SQUIRREL PERCHED on a log paused while chewing on some seeds. He watched as two tiny Never fairies zipped past him, side by side.

"Oh, Beck," one of the fairies said to the other as they flew. "Thank you so much for coming with me." She looked terribly worried. "We just don't know what to do. A baby raccoon turned up in the gardens this morning, and he ate all the strawberries out of Thistle's strawberry patch. And then he started digging up Rosetta's mint! We chased him off, but he didn't go far. Now he's sitting on a tree stump by Havendish Stream. He won't budge. And none of the other animal-talent fairies can understand a word he's saying!"

Beck smiled. "Don't worry, Latia," she said. They were nearing Havendish Stream. "We'll figure it out."

Latia breathed a sigh of relief. "Well, if any fairy in Never Land *can* figure it out, it's you, Beck!"

Every fairy in Never Land agreed: Beck was one of the finest animal-talent fairies in

Pixie Hollow. She loved being around animals, from the tiniest insects to the largest mammals. Oh, sure, snakes could be a little grumpy. Skunks were hard to read. And hawks, of course, were just plain dangerous. But all in all, she loved feeling a part of the animal world. Sometimes Beck secretly wished that *she* were an animal!

Like all the animal-talent fairies, Beck had a gift for talking to animals. Birdcalls, mouse squeaks, squirrel and chipmunk chatter—they were just noises to the other fairies. But to animal-talent fairies, those different noises held meaning. To them, animal sounds were as clear and easy to understand as words and sentences.

Beck was especially good at talking to baby animals, perhaps because she was so playful and lighthearted. She loved playing hide-and-seek with the young squirrels and having somersault contests with the baby hedgehogs. Even when an animal was too young to speak, Beck could understand it. Queen Clarion said Beck had empathy and could sense animals' emotions. When those emotions were strong enough, Beck felt them, too.

So when a baby raccoon parked himself on a stump and refused to move, everyone thought of Beck right away. The animal fairies sent Latia to fetch Beck because she was a forest-talent fairy and knew the quickest ways to get through Pixie Hollow.

An easy five-minute flight later, the two fairies came to Havendish Stream. A dozen animal-talent fairies were hovering around a tiny raccoon, who sat on a tree stump clutching a stalk of Rosetta's mint.

"Beck's here!" Latia called, and all the fairies turned.

"Oh, thank goodness!" cried Fawn, one of Beck's best friends. She drew Beck closer to the tree stump. "Beck, you've just got to help. This poor little fella won't budge. We don't even know where he *came* from." With a push from Fawn, Beck found herself right in front of the baby raccoon. He raised his head and whimpered.

"Hello there," Beck said in Raccoon. "I'm Beck. What's your name?"

The little raccoon let out another whimper. Then he buried his face in his paws and rubbed his nose in the stalk of mint he had picked from Rosetta's garden.

"Oh, don't cry!" Beck said. She flew up and stroked the top of the raccoon's furry head. The raccoon rocked back and forth—and Beck's lip started trembling. The baby raccoon was so sad and so scared that Beck was starting to feel sad, too. She straightened her back, cleared her throat, and forced herself to cheer up. If she didn't watch out, soon she'd be crying as hard as the little raccoon, and then where would the fairies be?

"Hey, now," said Beck, smiling. "Don't cry, my friend. Why would you cry when you could be playing a game with me?"

Raising his head, the little raccoon looked at Beck for the first time. She smiled encouragingly and patted his nose. "That's right," she said. "I know the perfect game for us to play. It's called Find the Fairy!"

With that, Beck took off at top speed. She looped around behind the raccoon and tapped him on the shoulder. "Here I am!" she cried. The raccoon squeaked in surprise and turned around, but Beck was already gone.

The little raccoon peered up at the sky, trying to find her. Meanwhile, Beck quietly landed by the stump and tiptoed around to the front, where the raccoon's paw rested on the edge. She reached up, tweaked his toe, and cried, "No, *here* I am!" then flew up to face him again.

The little raccoon let out a chittering noise: raccoon laughter. All the fairies smiled at each other. Beck had done it again!

Beck grinned. She was so glad that the

little fellow was feeling better. "That's a good game, isn't it?" she said. "Now let's start again. My name is Beck. What's wrong?"

There was a pause, and the fairies held their breath. Then the raccoon replied. To the fairies who didn't speak Raccoon, what he said sounded like "Grak!"

But Beck understood him.

"Lost!" was what the raccoon said. Beck realized that he was so young, he still spoke Raccoon baby talk. He stared at Beck with wide eyes. "Lost!" he said again.

"Oh, dear. Well, where do you live?" Beck asked.

"Live . . . ," the raccoon started.

"Yes?" Beck asked encouragingly.

"Live . . . ," he said again. He looked

down at the mint stalk he still held. He raised his paw and shook the mint at Beck. "Live *here*!" he said. "Live . . . in *mint*."

"Huh," said Beck, switching out of Raccoon. She looked at the fairies who were gathered around. Everyone looked as confused as she felt.

"What did he say?" asked Latia.

"He said . . . that he lives . . . in *mint*," Beck told her. "But that doesn't make any sense!"

"In mint?" replied Latia thoughtfully. "I wonder if he means— Oh, Beck! I know where he lives!"

"Remember when Rosetta planted her mint patch a few years ago?" Latia asked

Beck. They were flying through the woods, with the raccoon trailing after them. "Well, she asked me to find her some wild mint seeds from the forest, because she likes their flavor. So I got her some seeds from a big old wild mint patch at the base of a hollow tree right on the edge of Pixie Hollow. I just *bet* his family lives in that tree!"

"You must be right," agreed Beck. "That would explain why he was so interested in Rosetta's mint patch to begin with. It must have reminded him of—"

"*Home!*" cried the little raccoon, and took off running. Beck and Latia looked up, and sure enough, there was the big hollow tree. And playing in the mint leaves at the bottom of the tree was another baby raccoon. She was about the same age as

Beck's little friend—who was in such a hurry to get to the tree that he barreled into her. The two young raccoons tumbled in a heap at the foot of the hollow tree, squeaking happily.

It was obvious that the little raccoon was home.

Soon, it had all been sorted out. Beck explained everything to the baby raccoon's mother, who thanked her again and again. She even offered Beck an old, slimy leaf of cabbage (rotten cabbage is a delicacy to raccoons).

"Thank you so much, but it's really not necessary," Beck said. She waved good-bye to the baby raccoon, and then she and Latia flew off in the direction of the Home Tree.

As they were flying over a thicket, Beck spotted Grandmother Mole coming out of an underground tunnel. "Oh, Latia, why don't you go on without me?" Beck suggested. "I want to pay a visit."

Grandmother Mole was the oldest female mole in Never Land, and a very dear friend. She and old Grandfather Mole had no children or grandchildren of their own. But they were known throughout Pixie Hollow as Grandmother and Grandfather Mole.

"Hello, Grandmother," Beck said in Mole. She landed at the animal's side.

"Beck? Is that you?" asked Grandmother Mole in a series of grunts and nose whistles.

"Yes, it's me," Beck replied. "I was just

flying by and I saw you. How's everything underground?"

"Oh, just fine," Grandmother Mole replied. She told Beck all about the moles' latest tunneling projects. "But there's much more exciting news than that," she added. "One of our own just had babies—four beautiful and perfect baby moles. You should come by and see them sometime. You can teach them to play peekaboo."

Beck smiled. "That sounds wonder—"

Just then, old Grandfather Mole climbed out of the tunnel opening—and bumped right into Beck. "Oops!" he said with an embarrassed chuckle. He squinted in Beck's direction. "Pardon me, sir! Wasn't watching where I was going, I guess!" He chuckled again.

Then Grandfather Mole waddled off. Grandmother Mole giggled at his blunder—calling Beck "sir." Beck couldn't help giggling, too. All the moles were nearsighted. But Grandfather Mole, well, he was practically blind.

After saying farewell to Grandmother Mole, Beck flew east, to the Home Tree. She smiled as she flew. She was filled with a sense of well-being. Maybe it was from helping the baby raccoon get back home. Maybe it was the happy news of the baby moles' birth. Whatever it was, it made Beck feel, at that moment, that all was well with the world.

Then, just as Beck flew over the river, she heard it. A cry. A cry for her? Was someone calling her name? As she slowed, it got louder.

"Beck! Be-e-e-e-eck! Wait! Wait up!" the voice called.

Beck stopped and hovered in midair. Where was the call coming from? She looked to the left. She looked to the right.

She turned to look behind her—and saw a young hummingbird headed straight for her, at full speed. He was screaming at the top of his lungs. "Beck! Help! He-e-e-e-elp!"

2

THE YOUNG HUMMINGBIRD tried to put on the brakes. But it was too late. He was going too fast. Beck dodged to her right. Unfortunately, the hummingbird had the same thought. He dodged to his left—and smashed right into her.

The crash knocked Beck backward.

"Twitter!" Beck exclaimed in Bird. She shook her head, trying to clear it. "What in the world is going on?"

Twitter was no stranger to Beck. He was a high-strung little hummingbird. He was *so* high-strung that sometimes his mouth had a hard time keeping up with his brain.

"I'm s-s-sorry about that, B-B-Beck!" Twitter chirped in stuttering cheeps and peeps. He nervously darted to and fro in the air. His wings flapped so quickly, they seemed a blur to Beck's eyes. Still dazed from the midair crash, Beck was getting dizzy trying to keep her eye on Twitter. He stayed in the same place for only seconds at a time.

"I s-s-saw you f-f-flying by," Twitter said. "And it's j-j-just that you've g-g-got to help us—the hummingbirds. It's an e-e-emergency!"

Now over the shock of bumping into

Twitter, Beck smiled. How many times had she heard that word—"emergency"—from Twitter before? Twitter was a sweet, good, and earnest little bird, and he was better at playing tag than any other animal in Pixie Hollow. Beck liked him very much. But sometimes Twitter got overexcited for no reason.

He came looking for Beck whenever he needed help or advice. Usually, he was in a panic, as he was now. Once Beck found out the facts, she could explain why there was nothing for Twitter to worry about. Beck suspected that this was another one of those times.

She turned and headed east again, beckoning for Twitter to follow. "Come on, Twitter," she chirped. "I'm headed back to the Home Tree. Come with me. Along the way, you can tell me what's wrong."

Twitter hurried after Beck. "B-b-but you don't understand!" he called to her. "You have to c-c-come with me, back to the nest. Quick!"

Beck flew on. It was always a little hard for her to deal with Twitter when he was in a state. His nervousness could be contagious. She *knew* that everything was fine and that Twitter was upset about nothing. But his panic was so strong that it made her heart beat faster in sympathy.

It's nothing, she reminded herself. *He's all upset about nothing. It's never as bad as he thinks it is.*

She knew this from having dealt with Twitter's panicky episodes so many times before. One of the first times had been when Twitter was just a chick. He had seen apple blossom petals falling to the ground and had rushed to Beck in a panic.

"B-B-Beck! Come quick!" he had said. "It's snowing! It's not *supposed* to snow in Never Land!" It had taken Beck a while to reassure Twitter that the petals were just petals.

There had also been the time when Twitter had noticed that all the beautiful round yellow flowers he liked so much had disappeared. "Someone changed them into strange white puffy things," he said. "And they *fall apart.*"

Beck had explained to Twitter that they were dandelions, and that was how they spread their seeds. While he didn't like it—not one bit—he had finally calmed down.

So now Beck felt sure that Twitter's "problem" wasn't as big as he thought it was. "Okay, Twitter," she said. "What is it? I'm listening."

Twitter zigged this way and zagged that way in the air. "I'm telling you," he said, "it's an emergency! It's—" Twitter looked nervously over one wing, then the other. He flew right up to Beck's left ear and whispered, "It's the *chipmunks*."

"The chipmunks?" Beck said at a normal volume. "What about the chipmunks?"

"Shhh!" Twitter cringed and went on whispering. "Not so loud! They might be listening. They're everywhere." Twitter shot glances over both wings again. Then he continued. "And they're so grabby and strange. I think they have it in for all us birds. They come right up into the trees and shrubs. They gather all the seeds and acorns and berries in sight. And then, get this: they don't *eat* the stuff. They carry it away with them to their underground nests. You know what I think? I think they're *hoarding* all that food. They're taking it and

storing it somewhere—just so the birds *can't have it*." Twitter backed away from Beck's ear. He stopped whispering. "Why would they do that, Beck? Why?"

Beck listened carefully to everything Twitter said. She managed to keep a straight face the whole time. But when Twitter was done, she couldn't help it. She smiled. Then she giggled.

Twitter was confused. "What's so funny?" he asked Beck. "This is serious! This is an *emergency!*"

Beck fought back another giggle. "I'm sorry, Twitter," she said kindly. "I know you're upset. But there's no reason to be. The chipmunks mean no harm," she told him.

Twitter looked at her doubtfully.

"It's true," Beck went on. "Some animals, like birds, eat food as they find it. But other animals, like chipmunks, store some of the food they find. They save it until they need it. *Then* they eat it."

Twitter looked at Beck in surprise. "They do?" he asked.

Beck nodded. "Mm-hmm. It's nothing personal," she pointed out. "They don't have it in for the birds. They're just doing what they've always done. Besides, there's plenty of food to go around." Beck looked into Twitter's eyes. "Okay?" she asked.

Twitter thought it over for a second. "Okay!" he replied cheerfully. And just like that, Twitter was back to being a carefree little hummingbird. "Thanks, Beck!" he exclaimed as he zipped out of sight.

"You're welcome!" Beck called after him. She shook her head and smiled.

Just as quickly as he had come, Twitter was gone.

3

THAT AFTERNOON, Beck was sitting alone at the animal-talent table in the Home Tree tearoom. She was the first animal-talent fairy to get there—five minutes before tea-time. So as she waited for the others, Beck sipped peppermint tea.

She looked around the room. She waved to her friend Tink, sitting across the room at the pots-and-pans-talent table.

She saw pretty Rosetta fly into the room and join the fairies at the garden-talent table. She watched Dulcie, a baking-talent fairy, serve cookies to the hungry water-talent fairies.

The tearoom was one of the fanciest rooms in the Home Tree. The walls were hung with Never pale-grass wallpaper. The silver chandelier overhead sparkled and shone. The floral carpet was plush and colorful. And during the day, light flooded into the room through the floor-to-ceiling windows.

Beck loved the spot where the animal-talent fairies had their table, right next to one of the windows. She was gazing outside when Fawn sat down next to her. There was a bright purple stain on one shoulder of her dress.

Beck giggled. "What happened to you?" she asked Fawn.

Fawn reached for the teapot in the center of the table. She poured herself a cup of tea. "A berry fell on me," she explained. "After you took that raccoon home, I went to talk to this chameleon I know. He was feeling a little blue today." Fawn couldn't help smiling at her own silly joke. "Then I headed back here, and just as I landed in the courtyard—*splat!*" Fawn shrugged. "Just bad luck, I guess."

Beck shrugged, too. Never fairies were used to dodging all sorts of things falling from above. Raindrops falling from the sky. Leaves or branches falling from trees. Berries falling from shrubs. They had to be careful. But these things were just a bother—

not a big danger. Not like hawks, which could swoop out of the sky and carry away a Never fairy in a split second. That was why the fairies had scouts to watch for hawks. As for berries, they could make a big mess. But they hardly ever fell directly on a fairy.

Terra, Madge, and Finn were the next animal-talent fairies to come to the table. They helped themselves to tea. Dulcie flew over with a plate of star-shaped butter cookies. Everyone reached for one at the same time.

"Easy, easy!" Dulcie cried as she flew away. "There's plenty more where those came from."

"That's good," said Finn. She nodded toward the tearoom door. "Because here comes Cora. And it looks like she could use a pick-me-up."

Cora flopped into the last empty seat with a frustrated sigh. It was plain to see what was the matter. Bright purple juice soaked the top of her head. It dripped down her forehead. It dripped off the ends of her long, blond hair. It was smeared on the sides of her face, where she had tried to wipe it away.

"You, too, Cora?" Fawn asked. She pointed to the big purple splotch on her own dress.

Cora squinted at Fawn through the purple liquid. "Berry?" she said.

Fawn nodded.

"Yup," said Cora. "It came out of nowhere. Another one almost hit me, too."

Beck wrinkled her brow. "What a strange coincidence," she said. "Two fairies hit by berries in the same day. That doesn't happen very often."

On the other side of the table, Finn stared at something over Beck's shoulder. "Make that *three* fairies," said Finn.

"Huh?" said Beck. She turned to look.

Sure enough, a sparrow man at the art-talent table had a big purple stain on his left leg.

"I count four," said Madge. Across the room a decoration-talent fairy was wiping purple juice from the back of her neck.

"Uh . . . no," said Fawn. "Five." She nodded in the direction of the tearoom door. Lympia, a laundry fairy, had just flown in. Two purple splotches—one on her right arm and one on her left wing—showed where she had been hit.

What in the world was going on?

"This is no coincidence," said Beck. "Five fairies hit by berries in the same day? In the same *afternoon?*"

Just then, a loud *tap-tap*ping sound made all six animal talents jump in their seats. They turned toward the window. Outside, hovering, peeking in at them, was Twitter. He tapped again at the window with his long, thin beak.

Madge reached over and swung open the window. Twitter landed on the sill.

"B-B-Beck!" he chirped, short of breath. "Come qu-qu-quick! It's an emergency!"

All the animal-talent fairies smiled at Beck. They knew as well as she did how overexcited Twitter could get.

Madge patted Twitter gently on the head. "There, there, Twitter," she said in Bird. "It can't be all *that* bad."

Finn offered Twitter a cookie. "Here, try one of these," she said. "It'll make everything better."

But the animal talents knew that Beck was the only fairy with the patience to calm the little bird.

Twitter didn't take the cookie. "You don't understand!" he cried. Twitter hopped off the windowsill. He darted nervously from side to side. "A battle has broken out! B-B-Beck, you've got to do something! You've g-g-got to stop it!"

Beck squinted at the little bird. "A *battle?*" she said doubtfully. Even for Twitter, it sounded like a huge exaggeration—like something blown way out of proportion.

But the next thing Twitter said got the animal-talent fairies' attention.

"Yes, a battle!" he exclaimed. "A *berry* battle!"

4

Beck hurried out of the tearoom. She zipped through the Home Tree lobby and out the front door. She met Twitter outside the tearoom window.

"Twitter," Beck called to him, "what do you m—" Out of the corner of her eye, she spied a berry falling toward her. She dodged to her right. The berry just missed her left shoulder. "What do you mean, a berry battle?" she asked.

Twitter launched excitedly into a long explanation. But he was chirping almost as quickly as his wings were flapping. Beck could only understand bits and pieces.

"The chipmunks stole the nest!" cried Twitter. Then Beck caught something about the hummingbirds' deciding to fight back and "launching berries" and "defending our shrubs" and "keeping the chipmunks away." But the more Twitter explained, the more confused Beck got.

"Okay, okay, Twitter," Beck calmly interrupted him. "Let's do this: why don't you *show* me what you're talking about? Lead the way. I'll follow. And we'll get to the bottom of this together."

Without another word, Twitter turned and flew away. Beck hurried after him. At times, it was hard to keep up. He was fast. So was Beck. But unlike the smooth, graceful flight pattern of a Never fairy, the moves of a hummingbird are unpredictable.

Twitter would be headed straight for a tree trunk. Then, at the last possible moment, he would zigzag around it. He dodged branches—sailing over some, ducking under others. Beck followed Twitter's crazy path as they headed northeast from the Home Tree.

Before long, Twitter stopped and perched on the branch of a blackberry bush. Beck landed next to him. She looked around. Nothing seemed out of the ordinary. All around them, the forest was perfectly quiet.

Twitter sat silently, staring in front of him. Beck's curiosity bubbled over. "Twitter—" she began.

But Twitter shushed her. He pointed a wing toward the clearing at the foot of the blackberry bush. "Watch," he whispered.

So Beck sat quietly. She watched and waited. Sure enough, in a few moments, a chipmunk scampered out from behind a hawthorn tree. He looked to his left. He looked to his right. He looked up into the trees. Then he scampered across the clearing toward the blackberry bush. In the center of the clearing, the chipmunk stopped. He sat up on his hind legs. He sniffed the air. Beck could sense his nervousness—and his eagerness. He was determined to get his paws on some of those blackberries.

Suddenly, the blackberry bush seemed to spring to life. It was full of hummingbirds—young ones, old ones, male and female. Beck hadn't even noticed they were there, scattered throughout the bush, high and low.

Beck watched as the hummingbirds worked in pairs. One hummingbird bent back a branch. Another bird balanced a blackberry at the very tip of the branch.

Then, all at once, the hummingbirds let go of the branches. A storm of blackberries went flying in the direction of the clearing. A few went astray. Some hooked to the left, to the right, or backward. Some flew straight up into the air. Those came plummeting back down toward the blackberry bush. Beck saw one of them hit a hummingbird on the head.

But most of them flew directly at the chipmunk. He flinched as he saw the wave of berries headed right for him. He barely had time to turn away before they hit: one on his tail, one on the back of his head, and three more on his back. Several others were near misses.

Then, dripping berry juice, the chipmunk scampered out of the clearing—back

the way he had come. He disappeared behind the hawthorn tree.

"Hooray!" A round of cheerful hummingbird chirps rose from the blackberry bush.

It had all happened so fast that Beck hadn't had time to move. But now, shocked by what she had seen, she leaped off the branch. For once, Twitter was right. This *was* an emergency! Hummingbirds attacking a chipmunk with berries? What was going on here? She flew out in front of the blackberry bush. She turned to face the bush and hovered over the clearing.

"Stop! Stop!" she called in Bird. She held her hands up in front of her. "What are you doing? Why would you do that to that chipmunk?"

"Oh, good day to you, Beck," came a voice from the blackberry bush. Beck peered into the bush to see where—and who—it was coming from. Suddenly, from a low branch, out flew Birdie, one of the oldest hummingbirds in Pixie Hollow. Beck had known her for a long, long time. She was a no-nonsense, plainspoken old bird. "I see you've heard about our . . . *problem*," Birdie said, hovering next to Beck.

Beck shrugged. "Well, yes and no," she said. "I've heard that there *is* a problem. But I don't understand. What's going on?"

Birdie sighed a big sigh. "We have to be able to defend ourselves. Don't we?"

Now Beck was even more confused. "Defend yourselves?" she asked. "Defend yourselves from whom?"

"From the chipmunks, of course," Birdie replied. "They stole one of our nests! One minute it was here—right on one of these very branches." Birdie waved a wing at the blackberry bush. "The next minute it was gone! And a chipmunk was seen sniffing around that branch, just about that same time. All the hummingbirds nearby noticed him."

Beck thought over what Birdie had said. "Did anyone actually *see* the chipmunk take the nest?" she asked.

"Well," said Birdie, "no. But you know what chipmunks are like, Beck. They hoard. They stockpile. They hide away everything in sight. I'm sure they took it. They're very well-made nests, you know."

Birdie's chest puffed out with pride.

"Those chipmunks probably want to use it in one of their underground rooms—for padding or something. But they can't do that to us! They can't just steal one of our nests. And until they give it back or say they're sorry, they're not welcome in *our* shrubs. They can't help themselves to *these* berries. And if they get too close . . . well . . . just let them try!"

5

Beck didn't get very far with Birdie. She tried. She pointed out that there was probably an innocent explanation. Surely they could work it out, Beck said. Surely talking it over would work better than launching berries at them. But Birdie wouldn't listen. She was certain the chipmunks were thieves.

As for the chipmunks, they were just as

certain of something else: that the humming-birds were being mean. Beck had decided to get their side of the story. When she found them, the chipmunks were plotting their revenge against the birds. Uncle Munk, one of the chipmunk elders, and five others were gathered near the entrance to Uncle Munk's underground home.

Beck tried to get them to calm down. She told them what the hummingbirds had said.

"Of course we didn't take their nest!" insisted Uncle Munk in excited chipmunk chatter. "What would we want with one of their nests?"

"Great!" Beck replied. "Then it's just a misunderstanding. It can all be settled peacefully."

But the chipmunks were mad. Already, too many of them had gotten berried.

"Everywhere we go in Pixie Hollow, we get hit with berries," Uncle Munk said to Beck. "We have to gather the food we need. Otherwise, we'll starve. We have to be able to defend ourselves. Don't we?"

With that, the chipmunks went back to their planning. Uncle Munk gave the instructions.

"Here's what we do," he said. The other chipmunks leaned in to hear the plan. "We fan out in all directions. Keeping our distance, we circle the blackberry bush. Then we each start tunneling underground toward the bush. Oh, it'll be slow going. It could take days, even weeks. But when we get to the roots, we pop up from underground.

And we take the berries by force! Let's see them try to stop us!"

Beck couldn't believe what she was hearing. She had to put an end to this before it got entirely out of hand. She knew there had to be a way. But what was it? She couldn't help feeling very uneasy about the whole thing. If she didn't figure it out soon, this little quarrel was going to get much, much bigger!

Just then, a young chipmunk named Nan came running full speed around a tree trunk.

"Waaaaah!" screamed Nan as she ran. "Take cover! Take cover!"

Behind her, a shower of berries splattered on the forest floor, just missing her. Nan made a beeline for Uncle Munk's home. She dove headfirst down the entrance. As more berries landed closer and closer to them, the other six chipmunks followed Nan's lead. One by one, they dove for cover inside Uncle Munk's home. Beck was left alone, hovering over the entrance. She dodged one berry, then another. They both fell harmlessly on the forest floor.

But a third berry sailed high over her head. Beck watched it as it flew. It carved a wide, high arc in the air, then began its fall back to earth. At the same moment, an old mole came strolling around a tree trunk, directly into the berry's path.

It was Grandfather Mole. The berry dropped right on his head. *Splat!*

Grandfather Mole stopped in his tracks. He reached up to feel his head.

Finding it dripping wet, he turned and squinted in Beck's direction.

"Good day, sir," said the nearsighted old mole. "Awfully large raindrops we're having today, aren't we?"

6

Grandfather Mole's statement was not so far off. Because within a few days, it seemed to be raining berries—all over Pixie Hollow, all the time.

Some Never fairies started carrying their flower-petal umbrellas whenever they went outside. But, as every fairy soon found out, dainty flower-petal umbrellas didn't hold up very well to constant berry bombardment.

"Phooey!" said Silvermist, a water fairy, as she flew into the Home Tree lobby. Her water-lily umbrella was covered in berry juice. It also had been knocked inside out by the force of some direct hits. Silvermist shook the umbrella as she tried to close it. "This is the fourth umbrella I've gone through in two days!"

Beck overheard Silvermist and flew over to invite her to the umbrella exchange table. "Right this way," Beck said. She led Silvermist across the lobby. There Rosetta and three other garden fairies sat behind a tree-bark table. "You can drop off your ruined umbrella," Beck explained. "And you can pick up a new umbrella. The garden fairies will use your old one for seeds. So everyone wins!"

The umbrella exchange table had been Beck's idea. The Berry Battle was making big trouble for all the Never fairies, and she felt bad about that. She and the other animal-talent fairies were working as hard as they could to end the war. Over the past few days, between visits to Mother Dove, they had gone to see the hummingbirds and the chipmunks many times. They had tried to talk sense into them. But neither side was budging.

In the meantime, Beck wanted to do something to make things easier for the fairies. So she asked her garden-talent friends for help. They were experts at making flower-petal umbrellas. They were more than happy to pitch in. And now the idea of the umbrella exchange table seemed to

be taking off. They had only been set up for an hour, but already they had collected ten broken umbrellas.

One of the garden fairies helped Silvermist with her umbrella. Meanwhile, Rosetta noticed Beck glancing out the lobby window.

"Beck, we've got this under control," she said kindly. "I mean, if there's somewhere else you need to be . . ." She thought that Beck looked distracted.

She was right. Beck wanted to get outside. She wanted to check in with the animals. Maybe something had changed. Maybe they had called a truce. Or maybe today was the day Beck would think of some way to get them to stop fighting.

"Thanks, Rosetta," Beck replied. She smiled and waved good-bye to her friend as she flew toward the front door of the Home Tree. Then, at the door, she turned and flew back. She took a daisy-petal umbrella from the new-umbrella pile. "Mind if I borrow this?" she asked Rosetta.

Rosetta giggled. "Of course not," she replied.

And so, armed with the umbrella, Beck ventured outside. Almost right away, she heard a berry splatter on her open umbrella. Beck flew quickly through the berry shower. She dodged berries whenever she could. She only had to go a short distance out in the open—just as far as the big oak tree with the split trunk. From there, she could continue her trip underground by using the tunnels that were part of the animal-talent domain.

Long, long ago—so long ago that Mother Dove was the only one who could remember—the animal-talent fairies had built a huge system of tunnels stretching across Never Land. The fairies used them to get anywhere they wanted—without being seen and without setting foot outdoors.

Like all animal-talent fairies, Beck knew every inch of the tunnels like the back of her hand. But to other fairies, the tunnel system was a baffling maze. It wound through burrows, tree hollows, nests, and dens. A few had been abandoned, but many of them were home to families of animals.

Beck had decided that using the tunnels was the best way to travel while the Berry Battle raged. That way, she could stay dry and free of berry stains.

Beck set out first for the chipmunk camp. Diving through a small hole at the base of the big oak tree, she zipped down an underground tunnel that led toward Havendish Stream. She went aboveground to cross the stream, flying up a hollowed-out section of a maple tree, then down through the center of a dead limb that spanned the water. Then, back underground at a tunnel crossroads, she turned and headed due north through a series of empty fox dens.

On her way through the first den, she met Fawn coming in the opposite direction.

"Fawn!" Beck cried. Her face lit up at the sight of her friend. "I was on my way to see the chipmunks. Is there any news about the Berry Battle?"

Fawn frowned and shook her head. "Nothing good," she replied. "I just came from the hummingbird camp. They're still at it. No sign of either side letting up." Then Fawn's face brightened. "But now that I think of it, there is *one* piece of good news."

Beck's glow flared from her excitement. "I could use some cheering up," she replied eagerly. "What is it?"

"You know the chipmunks' plan to tunnel their way to the blackberry bushes?" Fawn asked. "Well, that plan backfired."

Beck looked confused. "What do you mean 'backfired'?" she asked Fawn. "What happened?"

Just then, they heard a muffled scratching sound. It was coming from the tunnel that led north out of the fox den.

Fawn nodded in the direction of the sound. "That will answer your question," she told Beck.

Puzzled, Beck flew over to the tunnel opening. She peered down the dim passage. The sound was getting louder . . . and closer.

As Beck peered farther into the tunnel, a large paw suddenly punched through the floor. It tore at the edges of the hole it had created, widening the opening. Then a furry head with a longish snout and tiny, beady eyes poked into the tunnel and looked around.

It was Grandmother Mole.

She spotted Beck and Fawn hovering in the doorway to the fox den.

"Oops!" said Grandmother Mole. She turned to talk to someone behind her.

"Back up! Retreat!" she said. "False report! This isn't a chipmunk tunnel. It's the fairies' tunnel. Abort mission! Repeat: abort mission!"

Beck was bewildered. She had no clue what kind of "mission" Grandmother Mole was leading. But she had a hunch it had something to do with the Berry Battle. And that could mean only one thing.

The moles had taken sides.

BECK'S HUNCH TURNED out to be right.
The moles had sided with the hummingbirds in the Berry Battle.

"But why?" Beck asked Grandmother
Mole. She and Fawn hovered on either side
of the old mole in the dim tunnel. "Why
would you want to get mixed up in all this?"

Grandmother Mole snorted. "Well,"
she said, "we didn't want to. But then those

nasty chipmunks started digging all over the place. They started tunneling around all the blackberry bushes in Pixie Hollow. They bulldozed right through *our* tunnels. That's not nice. Plus, they caused a lot of damage. Our tunnels had to be fixed after the chipmunks plowed through." Grandmother Mole shrugged. "We had to do *something*."

From the look on Fawn's face, Beck could tell she already knew what that "something" was. Beck was afraid to ask. But she asked anyway. Grandmother Mole explained how the moles had been . . . *fiddling* with the chipmunks' tunnels.

"When they quit digging for the day, we build lots of side tunnels off their tunnels," she said. "They come back the next day, and they get confused. They can't figure out where they left off." Grandmother Mole stifled a giggle. "We've got them so turned around, they don't know which way is up."

Beck sighed. She didn't like the fact that there were now *more* animals involved in the Berry Battle. She shook her head slowly.

"So now it's the hummingbirds and the moles against the chipmunks," she said sadly.

At Beck's side, Fawn cleared her throat. "Actually, Beck," she said, "now it's the hummingbirds and the moles against the chipmunks and the *mice*."

Beck hurried on to the chipmunks' camp near Uncle Munk's home. She didn't want to believe what Fawn had said: that the mice had entered the war, too.

But when Beck reached the chipmunks' camp, she found that it was true. Little Nan, the young chipmunk whom Beck had seen diving for cover into Uncle Munk's home a few days earlier, brought her up to date. Nan was a very shy, quiet little chipmunk. She didn't speak much to the other chipmunks—let alone to the Never fairies. So when she and Beck had first met, many moons before, it had taken Beck a long time to win Nan's trust.

Now, however, little Nan felt as comfortable with Beck as she did with her own family.

"The hummingbirds accidentally hit a baby mouse with a berry," Nan explained to Beck. "Oh, they've hit plenty of other mice. Their aim is not always so good, you know. But this was a baby. The poor thing was completely drenched—and scared. After that, the mice took our side."

Beck pulled Nan aside, away from the worst of the fighting. They sat in the shelter of a hollow log. From there, they could see the animals battling it out.

It wasn't a pretty scene. To their left, the hummingbirds launched berries from the blackberry bush. To their right, chipmunks filled the branches of a hawthorn tree. Mice scurried to and fro in the clearing between. They collected any berries that fell to the ground still intact. Then, scurrying

into the hawthorn tree, they passed those berries off to the chipmunks. The chipmunks balanced those on their tails. Then they flung them back at the hummingbirds.

Beck pointed at a sparrow flying toward the chipmunks in the hawthorn tree. He was carrying a berry in his beak.

"What's that sparrow doing?" Beck wondered aloud.

Nan followed Beck's gaze. "Oh," she replied. "I forgot to mention: the sparrows are on the hummingbirds' side. So are the chickadees and the cardinals."

Beck peered up into the air. Flocks of birds were dive-bombing the hawthorn tree. Berries were flying and falling everywhere. The Berry Battle was getting completely out of hand!

In the midst of it all, little Twitter flew right past Beck and Nan. He was so busy dodging falling berries that he didn't see them.

"Twitter!" Beck called out to him.

Twitter looked around, trying to figure out who was calling him.

"Over here!" Beck called. "Inside the log!"

Twitter saw her and flew over to the hollow log. He landed inside, next to Beck. "Whew!" he said, shaking some berry juice off one wing. "It's g-g-getting harder and harder to g-g-get around out there!"

That was when Twitter looked up. He saw Nan standing on the other side of Beck.

"Oh!" said Twitter, staring at Nan. "It's a ch-ch-chipmunk!" he said to Beck.

Beck smiled. She stepped out of the way so that Twitter and Nan could face each other.

"That's right, Twitter," said Beck in Bird. "It's a chipmunk. Her name is Nan." Beck turned and spoke in Chipmunk to Nan. "Nan, this is Twitter."

There was a long, awkward silence. Twitter stared at Nan. Nan stared at Twitter. Their families were fighting against each other. They both felt as if maybe *they* should be fighting. Maybe that was what they were *supposed* to do.

But what do you know? Neither of them particularly felt like fighting.

8

BECK WATCHED TWITTER and Nan eye each other curiously. When their eyes met, they both looked away bashfully. Twitter stared at the ground. Nan tugged at her ear. Then, slowly, their gazes crept toward each other again.

It was Twitter who asked the first question. "Where does she live?" he chirped at Beck.

Beck pointed to the east. "Over there," she replied. "Past the hawthorn tree, over the stream, in a little burrow."

"Where does he live?" Nan asked Beck.

Beck pointed west. "In a big mulberry bush over that way."

"Is he your friend?" asked Nan.

"Yes, he is," replied Beck. "And guess what? He loves to play hide-and-seek." Beck knew that Nan also loved to play hide-and-seek. And she knew that no one had played any games at all since the Berry Battle had begun.

"Really? Do you think he'd play hide-and-seek with me?" Nan asked shyly.

Beck turned to Twitter. "Nan wants to know if you'll play hide-and-seek with her," she said.

Twitter jumped a few inches off the
ground and hovered in midair. "Yeah!" he
replied. He was so excited, he flew an
upside-down loop. Beck didn't have to
translate that. Nan understood. She put
her paws over her eyes. Twitter flew down
to the other end of the log and hid behind
a leaf. Nan opened her eyes and started

looking. Just as she reached the leaf that Twitter was hiding behind, he popped up and flew off to the other side of the hollow log. Nan followed him.

Beck giggled as she watched them go. Twitter and Nan were so excited about making friends, they had forgotten all about her. She turned and looked out toward the berry battlefield. She sighed. *If only the grown-up animals could put aside their differences as easily as the young ones,* she thought.

In the distance, she spotted Terence, a fairy-dust-talent sparrow man. He was struggling to fly through the shower of berries. In his arms he carried a dried minipumpkin canister full of fairy dust.

Terence gave out the daily doses of

fairy dust to the Never fairies. Each fairy got one level teacupful every day. It was an important job. Without fairy dust, fairies could only fly about a foot at a time. But with fairy dust, they could fly as long and as far as they wanted.

Beck guessed that Terence was on his way back to the Home Tree from the mill. He was trying to dodge berries as he flew. Beck took off to see if she could help him. But as she did, she saw a large berry fall right on Terence's canister and knock it out of his hands. The canister fell to the ground. Fairy dust spilled everywhere.

"Oh, Terence," Beck said when she reached his side. "Are you all right?"

Terence looked very unhappy. "I'm fine," he answered glumly. "But this fairy dust is wasted." He looked down at the glittery powder on the forest floor. Beck followed his gaze. A thin layer of fairy dust had fallen on an anthill. As she watched, all the ants that had been sprinkled with dust took to the air and flew around. Then she noticed a couple of spiders and an earthworm hovering in the air next to her.

Beck couldn't help laughing at the strange sight. "At least someone's getting some use out of it," she said.

Terence wasn't amused. "Yeah," he said. "But now— Oh, watch out!" He pulled Beck out of the path of a falling blackberry. "Now I have to make another trip back to the mill." He sighed a heavy sigh. "I'll tell you, Beck. This Berry Battle is out of control!"

"You don't know the half of it!" Beck

replied. She told Terence about the moles, the mice, the sparrows, the chickadees, and the cardinals. "Now *they're* all mixed up in this silly spat, too!"

Terence shook his head in disbelief. "What do you think would get them to stop fighting?" he asked.

At that very moment, Beck heard Nan and Twitter—or felt them with her animal-talent sense. Later, she couldn't exactly say which. Had she *heard* their cries for help? Or had she just sensed that they were in grave danger? Either way, she knew without a doubt that she had to find them. They needed her—and fast!

Beck wheeled around. She squinted to see across the clearing. Her eyes found the hollow log where she had last seen the youngsters. What she saw made her gasp aloud.

A large hawk was perched atop the log. He bent over to poke his sharp beak into the hollow interior.

Hiding inside the log, cornered, were Twitter and Nan.

9

BECK SPRANG INTO action. She flew straight for the hawk, across the berry battle-field.

"Hold your fire!" she shouted in both Bird and Chipmunk as she flew down the front lines of the Berry Battle. "I repeat, hold your fire!"

Beck knew she couldn't fight off the hawk herself. She would need help—and lots of it. But none of the chipmunks or hummingbirds had seen that Nan and Twitter were in trouble. So as she flew, Beck waved her arms wildly. She threw herself in front of flying berries. She did everything she could think of to get the animals' attention.

She pointed at the hawk. "Stop fighting and look!" she shouted.

Slowly but surely, the warring animals noticed Beck. Hummingbirds and chipmunks alike froze in the middle of berry launches. A few moles who had popped up from underground watched Beck fly by. Mice looked up from their berry-collection duties. Sparrows, chickadees, and cardinals circled in the air. They were curious to see what Beck was shouting about.

They all looked where she was pointing. They saw the hawk. And they saw Nan and Twitter.

All at once, the Berry Battle came to a halt.

Beck reached the log first. Now she could see why Twitter and Nan were cornered. The hawk had smashed in one end of the hollow log, blocking the exit. That left only the one open end, which he was guarding. He was hunched over, peering upside down into the log. He couldn't go in after the young animals. The log was too small. Instead, he waited for them to try to escape.

Beck didn't stop to think. She swooped past the hawk's face, flying dangerously close to his curved beak. She got his attention. She flew up, behind his head. The

hawk sat upright as his eyes followed her. She circled his head. She didn't really have a plan. She just hoped to draw his attention away from the youngsters. If she could distract him long enough, maybe they could get away.

The hummingbirds saw what Beck was trying to do and caught on. Within moments, dozens of hummingbirds swarmed around the hawk. They poked at the top of his head with their long, pointy beaks. They flew in front of his face, zigging and zagging.

Their tactics had an effect. The hawk was getting mad. He lunged at a hummingbird and snapped his beak just millimeters from her wing. He flapped his wings out wide, as if trying to shoo the tiny birds and the fairy away. The wind from the hawk's flapping blew some hummingbirds off course. A few others were hit by his wings and knocked to the ground. They sat there dazed for a moment before they were able to get up and take to the air again.

But through it all, the hawk didn't budge from the log.

Other birds moved in to take the place of the hummingbirds. Sparrows, chickadees, and cardinals circled over the hawk's head. Then, one by one, they dive-bombed the hawk with berries. Many made direct hits. Several berries hit the hawk on the head. One hit him right between the eyes.

But the berries didn't bother the hawk. He barely noticed them. They were tiny to a bird of his size. In fact, even as the birds dropped berries on him, the hawk went back to peering into the log.

The animals had to find another way to distract him!

The chipmunks launched the next attack. They scurried onto tree branches hanging directly over the log. Then, throwing caution to the wind, two chipmunks dove onto the back of the hawk's head. He stood bolt upright on the log. He raised his right wing and brushed at his head, trying to get the chipmunks off. The chipmunks clung for dear life. As long as they could hang on to the back of the bird's head, they were safe from his sharp beak and talons.

Meanwhile, behind the hawk's back, Uncle Munk had sneaked up to the log. Hugging one side of it, he crept closer and closer to the open end. Now, while the hawk was distracted, he scurried up to the opening. He peeked around the corner and into the log.

"Psst!" he whispered to Nan and Twitter. "Come on! Follow me! The coast is clear. But we don't have much time!"

Even though he couldn't understand Uncle Munk's words, Twitter zipped forward.

But Nan didn't follow.

"Nan!" Uncle Munk whispered to her from the end of the log. "Come on! Now's our chance!"

Nan was frozen with fear. She couldn't move. She huddled against the back of the log, trembling, her eyes wide.

"You go ahead!" Uncle Munk whispered to Twitter, waving him on. Twitter hesitated. He looked back and forth from Nan to Uncle Munk. He didn't want to leave his new friend behind. But Uncle Munk was a grown-up. Twitter felt he should do what Uncle Munk wanted.

So Twitter flitted past Uncle Munk and out of the log. The hawk, still trying to shake the chipmunks off his head, didn't even see him fly past. Within seconds, Twitter was safe. He landed on a blackberry branch. The hummingbirds flocked to him to make sure he was okay.

"I'm f-f-fine," he told everyone. "But Nan . . ."

Nan was still trapped inside the log. Uncle Munk stood at the opening, trying to convince her to make a break for it.

"You can do it, Nan," Beck heard Uncle Munk say. "Just put one paw in front of the other. Come toward me."

He was so focused on Nan, he didn't notice that the hawk had shaken the chipmunks off. They ran for cover as the giant bird turned back to the log. He spotted Uncle Munk.

Beck and all the animals gasped.

"Uncle Munk!" Beck called. "Run!"

Uncle Munk heard Beck. He looked

up. The hawk's eyes were glued to him. The bird leaned in. His shadow fell over Uncle Munk. Then, in one sudden, lightning-fast movement, the hawk lunged at Uncle Munk. The chipmunk dodged the bird's hooked beak, wheeled around, and scurried away.

The hawk leaned over to look inside the log once more. Seeing Nan still there, he settled down to wait her out. He showed no sign of giving up.

The animals had to try something else. Birdie the hummingbird had an idea. As Beck had done, she swooped past the hawk's face to get his attention. Then she landed on the ground a few feet in front of the log. She hopped along, dragging one wing behind her. The hawk watched her, cocking his head. He leaned forward to get a closer look.

"She's pretending she's hurt!" Beck said to Uncle Munk. "She's figuring that hawks go for the easiest prey first. Young animals are easy targets. But injured animals are even easier. She's trying to lure the hawk off the log—to get him to go for her."

What Birdie was doing was terribly dangerous. She was risking her own life to save Nan's.

Beck and Uncle Munk watched as Birdie turned her back on the hawk. Slowly, slowly, she hopped away from the log. The hawk leaned over again to look in at Nan. Then he looked up at Birdie. He looked back and forth between his two choices of prey. He seemed torn—between the trapped chipmunk he couldn't reach and the hurt hummingbird inching away from him. He had to decide.

The hawk spread his wings and leaped off the log. He soared the short distance to Birdie and got ready to drop onto the little bird. But at the last possible moment, Birdie took to the air. She flew a few feet, landed again, and continued hopping along, dragging her wing. The hawk flew after her and pounced again. Again, Birdie took off at the last second. She flew several feet, landed, and hopped. The hawk followed her.

"Now is our chance," whispered Uncle Munk. He sprang into action. With the hawk out of the way, he dashed over to the log. He leaped inside and ran to the back.

"Nan, come with me! You can do it!" he told her.

With a little encouragement and a lot of shoving, Uncle Munk got Nan out of the log. They ran away as fast as they could. Within seconds, they were safe, hidden behind the trunk of an oak tree.

"Birdie!" Beck called out. "Birdie, they're clear!"

Birdie heard Beck's call and knew that Nan was safe. So when the hawk pounced again, she took to the air. This time, she sped away.

The confused hawk watched her fly out of his reach. Then, remembering the trapped little chipmunk, he flew back to the log. Peering inside, he saw that Nan was gone. He checked on both sides of the log to make sure she wasn't hiding nearby. He looked around for other prey. But all the animals and Beck were safely out of sight.

Out of ideas, the hawk gave up and flew away.

All around the clearing, the animals breathed sighs of relief. They had outwitted the hawk. They had saved Nan and Twitter.

And they had done it by working together.

THE ANIMALS STAYED hidden for a few
minutes to make sure the coast was really
clear. Then, one by one, chipmunks, mice,
hummingbirds, sparrows, chickadees, moles,
and cardinals came out of their hiding
places. Slowly and warily, they gathered
in the clearing. They made a wide circle
around Nan and Twitter, Uncle Munk,
Birdie, and Beck.

"Are you two all right?" Beck asked the youngsters. They looked unharmed. But Beck could sense that they were still getting over their fear—especially Nan.

"I'm okay," Twitter replied.

He was strangely calm—none of his usual flitting around. Maybe this *real* emergency had sapped all his nervous energy, thought Beck. If so, the change was sure to be temporary. Beck expected he'd be back to his old excitable self in no time.

"Are *you* okay, Nan?" Twitter asked his new friend. Beck translated for him.

Nan nodded but didn't speak.

"She'll be fine," Uncle Munk said cheerfully. He looked up at Birdie. "And it's thanks to you, old bird. What would we have done if you hadn't stepped in and

saved her?" Uncle Munk looked down at the ground bashfully. "You risked everything for Nan. How can we thank you?"

Beck told Birdie what Uncle Munk had said. Birdie brushed off the praise with a backhand wave of her wing. "Nonsense," she replied. "*You're* the one who got Twitter safely out of that log. You are due as much credit as I am." She turned to Beck. "And you! What if you hadn't been here, Beck? We were all so wrapped up in our"—Birdie paused—"*argument*. We might not have seen that the little ones were in trouble . . . until it was too late."

Beck smiled a big smile. Her glow flared with a mixture of embarrassment and pride. "Oh, don't mention it," she said. But secretly, Beck was very glad to think she might have been of some help. Especially after days and days of trying to end the Berry Battle—with no luck.

"I'm just glad this whole thing is over," Beck said with a chuckle. She looked at Uncle Munk. She looked at Birdie. Her chuckle trailed off. "It *is* over, isn't it?" she asked them, first in Chipmunk, then in Bird. "The Berry Battle, I mean."

Birdie shifted her weight from one foot to the other. "Well," she said, "there *is* the small matter of the nest." She looked over at Uncle Munk. "The missing nest, that is. I *do* think it would be nice if they would return it."

Uncle Munk stared at Beck with wide eyes while she translated. "But we didn't even take that nest!" he cried. "Honestly!

I don't know why they think we did."

Birdie squinted at Uncle Munk. She was trying to decide whether she believed him. Uncle Munk stared back at her. Beck hovered nervously between them. *Oh, no,* she thought. *Here we go again.*

No one spoke for many long moments. The whole clearing was silent. All the other animals waited to hear what would happen next.

Then, on the outer ring of the circle of animals, there was a slight commotion.

"Oh, pardon me," came a friendly voice from the midst of the hubbub.

Beck watched as the animals in that area shifted suddenly to the left and to the right. They seemed to be clearing a path for someone.

"Oh, excuse me," said the voice. "Oof! Pardon me. Oh! Bit of a gathering here, eh?"

The front row of animals parted. Out from behind them strolled old Grandfather Mole. He had stumbled and bumped his way through the crowd. Now, moseying past Beck, he tipped his hat. "Good day, sir!" he said to her. "Somewhat crowded in the forest today, isn't it?"

It took a few moments for Beck to notice that his hat was not a hat at all. It was an upside-down, hollowed-out mass of moss, plant bits, and spiderwebs.

It was a hummingbird nest.

"Um, Grandfather Mole?" she called. She flew over and landed facing him. "If you please," she said, "where did you get that . . . *thing* on your head?"

All around Beck, the animals realized what it was. They gasped and pointed at Grandfather Mole's head. Birdie's beak hung open.

"What?" Grandfather Mole said. "Do you mean my hat?" He reached up and took it off. He held it out at arm's length. He squinted at it. "Isn't it a fine hat? I found it a few days ago. I was out for a walk. I strolled by that blackberry bush over yonder." Grandfather Mole pointed to the hummingbirds' bush—the very bush that the missing nest had been in.

"This hat was on the ground underneath it. Oh, naturally, I looked around to see if anyone might have dropped it. But there was no one in sight. So I picked it up and tried it on. It fit perfectly!" He put the nest back on his head. "See?" he said, modeling it for Beck. "I'm wearing it out for the first time this afternoon. With all this strange weather we've been having, it's come in very handy," Grandfather Mole added.

Beck could not believe her ears. She looked over at Birdie and Uncle Munk. They seemed equally amazed. Could it be? Had the nest actually just *fallen* out of the bush? Had Grandfather Mole had it the whole time? Had the forest really been divided over a silly misunderstanding?

"Well, good day to you," said Grandfather Mole as he continued on his walk. He strolled out of the clearing. The animals watched him walk away with a hummingbird nest on his head.

Then, suddenly, Beck and all the animals—hummingbirds, chipmunks, moles, mice, sparrows, chickadees, and cardinals—began to laugh.

They laughed because they hadn't laughed in days. They laughed at their memories of each other dripping in berry juice. They laughed from relief that it was over.

And they laughed because Grandfather Mole looked very silly with a nest for a hat.

Their laughter was so loud that several Never fairies in the Home Tree, a fair distance away, heard the sound.

It was the sound of the end of the Berry Battle.

The Trouble with Tink

Just then, they heard a metallic creaking sound. Suddenly—*plink, plink, plink, plink!* One by one, tiny streams of water burst through the damaged copper. The pot looked more like a watering can than something to boil dye in.

"Oh!" Violet and Terence gasped. They turned to Tink, their eyes wide.

Tink felt herself blush, but she couldn't tear her eyes away from the leaking pot. She had never failed to fix a pot before, much less made it worse than it was when she got it.

The thing was, no fairy ever failed at her talent. To do so would mean you weren't really talented at all.

Vidia and the Fairy Crown

All eyes turned toward Vidia, who crossed her arms and shifted her weight from one foot to the other. She scowled across the fairy circle at Rani and Tink.

"Well?" said Queen Ree, turning to look at Vidia. "Is that true? Did you say that, Vidia?"

"I said that I wasn't coming to the party," Vidia replied. "I think my exact words were 'unless, of course, you need someone to fly in and snatch that gaudy crown off high and mighty Queen Ree's head.' "

The crowd gasped. To say such a thing—and right in front of the queen herself!

Lily's Pesky Plant

Suddenly, something crashed through the leaves over her head. Lily gasped and flew for cover between the roots of a nearby tree. Had a hawk swooped at her? Trembling, Lily peered out from behind the root and scanned the forest.

But there was no sign of a hawk. The forest was still and quiet. Lily looked over at the possum fern and saw that its leaves had uncoiled and turned brown. It had heard the noise and was playing dead.

Then Lily saw something that made her gasp again. In the spot where she had just been standing sat a strange seed.

Coming in May 2006

Rani in the Mermaid Lagoon

Rani's heart thumped wildly in her chest. She knew that the Mermaid Lagoon held many dangers. There were lightning eels, which gave off an electric shock whenever something touched them. There were the small but fierce saberfish, which had teeth that were longer than their fins. And there were tusked Never sharks. These sharks usually left others alone. But when they were angry, they could be ferocious. And, Rani thought, there were probably other dangers, too. Ones she hadn't heard about.

Suddenly, Rani felt certain that the mermaids needed her help.

Believing is just the beginning...

Come on a magic journey with Disney Fairies . . .
all it takes is faith, trust, and a little bit of pixie dust!

The Trouble with Tink

Vidia and the Fairy Crown

Lily's Pesky Plant

Beck and the Great Berry Battle

COLLECT THEM ALL!

Look for these and other *Fairies* books
coming soon wherever books are sold.

RANDOM HOUSE
CHILDREN'S BOOKS

Disney Fairies

Believing is just the beginning...

The Trouble with Tink

Vidia and the Fairy Crown

Lily's Pesky Plant

Beck and the Great Berry Battle

Which Disney Fairy Are You?

Are you proud and feisty like Tink?
Or sly and sarcastic like Vidia?
Do you love animals as much as Beck?
Or would you rather spend all day
in a garden like Lily?

Tell us which Disney Fairy
you are most like and why.
ENTER NOW!

One grand-prize winner
will win a trip for four
to a Disney World Theme Park!

All entries must be received by July 31, 2006.

Log on to **www.randomhouse.com/kids/disney**
for complete rules and details.

Disney PRESS

RANDOM HOUSE
CHILDREN'S BOOKS